# Auctioned to the Cowboy

## Highest Bidder

## Hope Ford

Auctioned to the Cowboy © 2023 by Hope Ford

Editor: Kasi Alexander

Cover Design: Cormar Covers

# COLE

"So?" I ask with my arms crossed over my chest.

I sent two ranch hands over to the Reid Ranch earlier today, but they're back now, and I barely let them get out of the truck before I'm asking them questions.

Rick shrugs his shoulders. "It's no different than the last time we went, boss. Amos is letting that ranch fall apart all around him."

Travis nods in agreement. "Yeah. I mean, we did what we could, but there's only so much we can get done in one day. We mended fences, Rick patched some holes in the roof of the barn, and then we both worked on the tractor until we were able to get it running. We were able to fix it, but who knows how long for. It's almost as old as Amos."

I ask in a cool tone, not wanting to give anything away, "What about Sassy? Did you see her while you were there?"

Rick leans over and smacks Travis in the back of the head as he smirks at him. "Yeah, we saw Sassy. Travis got to work with her the whole day."

Travis has a big goofy grin on his face, and I can feel my stomach turn. This can't be good. "Oh yeah? You worked with Sassy today?"

He nods his head up and down. "Yeah. I swear she works harder than most men."

I'm about to let out a breath of relief. I don't know what I was thinking, but-

"Yeah, she's always in those big shirts and jeans. Today she was wearing some kind of tank top. I swear, I had no idea, but she's got a nice set of tits-"

I stomp toward him, ready to pounce. I grab the front of his sweat-stained shirt and pull him to me. "Did you touch her?"

His mouth falls open, and Rick obviously wants no part of this because he takes a few steps back. Travis doesn't answer me, and I see red. Gripping his shirt tighter, I pull him toward me until I'm spitting the words in his face. "I said did you touch her?"

Travis shakes his head quickly. "No, of course not. I was just looking-"

I'm towering over him, and it wouldn't take much for me to punch him in the face for even thinking that it's okay to talk about Sassy this way. "No looking. No talking about her body. Nothing. So help me, Travis, if I hear that you disrespect her again, I'll kill you, and no one will find the body. You got me?"

Travis' eyes are round as saucers. "Yes, yes. No looking... no talking. I got it."

The man is a big guy but nowhere as big as me. Right now, it doesn't matter how big he is because I'm not going to let anyone talk about Sassy that way.

I release him, pushing him away from me in disgust. "Get to work."

I'm breathing heavily, trying to get myself under control. I wait for him to argue because it's already after dark, and he's put in a full day of work. But the way he's looking at me right now, he'll go muck stalls or something to get away from me. "Sure thing, boss."

He runs to the barn, and I turn to Rick. He's standing a good fifteen feet from me now. If he knew what was good for him, he'd walk away too. "What is it, Rick? You got something to say?"

He shakes his head and then lets out a breath. "Well, uh, it's, uh..."

He keeps stammering, and I force myself to relax. Rick is a good guy and has never given me any problems. Obviously there's something on his mind. I count to ten before I ask again, my voice sounding way calmer than I'm feeling, "What is it, Rick? You got something on your mind?"

He nods. "Yeah, well, I mean, it's obvious that Sassy means something to you..."

His voice trails off, and my hands fist at my sides. "If you're about to tell me that you plan on asking her out-"

He cuts me off. "No, gosh no, boss. I just thought you'd want to know..."

His voice trails off again, and I take five steps toward him. I have to give it to him. He doesn't back away. He stands firmly in his spot, watching my every move. "You thought I'd want to know what?"

His voice trembles, but he manages to get it out. "There's something wrong. I mean, she's always happy... always. And she tried to laugh and smile today. She tried to act like everything was okay, but I could tell something was off. She was... upset."

I train my eyes on his. "Did you ask her about it?"

He frowns. "No, I didn't. We don't really talk about stuff besides what we're supposed to do when we go there. I didn't feel right asking her something personal, but I thought you'd want to know."

I clasp my hand on his shoulder, and he flinches. I force a smile on my face even though it's the last thing I want to do. I'm known as a grump... fuck, it's more than that. I'm known as an ass. I'm fair, and I pay my guys well, but they have to put up with my attitude to get it. Even though I'm set in my ways and don't plan on changing, I do appreciate Rick sticking his neck out for Sassy. "Thanks, Rick. I'll talk to her."

He lets out a big breath, and I release him. "Uh, okay, I'm going to go make sure the animals are all good. See you in the morning, boss."

"Yeah, see you," I mumble, already lost in thought.

I haven't seen Sassy since last week. I've forced myself to stay away from her and her father's ranch. Since the day she turned eighteen three years ago, my feelings for her have changed. I shouldn't be thinking the thoughts I've had for her, and I thought by putting some distance between us, I would be able to forget about her. But that isn't the case. If anything, I think about her more.

Her father is struggling. His ranch has been in the family for some hundred-odd years, and he's doing what he can to keep it, but getting older is getting the best of him. Sassy is doing what she can. And Travis is right: She works harder than most men, but there's only so much she can do when it's all left up to her. They don't have the money to make the improvements they need, but Amos won't take any money from me. He's a stubborn man and refuses any kind of handout.

I shove my hand through my hair in frustration. I'm assuming the ranch is what's bothering Sassy, but I can't guarantee it. Heck, I've avoided her and have no idea what's going on with her. Some asshole could be bothering her, for all I know.

Just the thought that some man is upsetting her makes me want to go over to her ranch right now and set whoever it is straight.

I pull out my phone. I never text Sassy even though I've had her number plugged into my phone for years. I find her in my favorites and type out a text. *Did Rick and Travis do okay for you? Give you any problems?*

I stare at my phone and hold my breath when I see the bubbles that she's typing something back. *Cole? Everything was fine. You didn't have to send them over AGAIN. I've got this handled.*

I shift my weight from one foot to the other. I don't know why, but it bothers me that she answered that way. What does that mean, she's got it handled? I type out a text. *I'm just being neighborly.*

I hit send and wait. The bubbles appear, disappear, come back on and then off again. I wait a full five minutes before the text comes back. *Thanks.*

I scrunch my nose up. Thanks? It took her that long for one word? *You don't have to thank me. Everything else okay? Anyone bothering you?*

I hit send before I can talk myself out of it. I've never pried into her business, but I know I won't sleep if someone is bothering her, and not knowing is killing me.

I wait a full five minutes and say fuck it. I hit dial on her name and put the phone to my ear. When she answers, she's breathless. "Lo?"

"Hey, Sassy. You okay?"

She is silent for a minute, and I pull the phone from my ear to see if she hung up. When I see the timer going, I put it back to my ear and repeat her name. "Sassy."

"What's going on, Cole?"

She sounds defensive, and that's not what I want. Sassy has always been independent, and she won't appreciate me snooping into her life even if I'm only worried about her. I can't tell her what Rick confessed, so I try to just get her talking. "Nothing's going on. I was just wanting to check on you. Everything okay over there?"

"Yeah, everything's fine."

I slap my hand to my forehead. She says she's fine, but it's not enough. "No one bothering you?"

She draws in a deep breath. "Who would be bothering me?"

I don't know what to answer, and she asks again. "Huh, Cole? Who would be bothering me?"

I sit down on the top step of my porch. "No one... I was just calling to make sure you're okay. That's all. Amos doing okay?"

She sighs, and I can hear the exhaustion in her voice. "He has his good days and his bad days."

"Aww, honey. Was today a bad day?"

"Yeah, uh, he doesn't know who I am some days, and today was one of those days."

I can hear the pain in her voice. I knew Amos was getting older. The last few times I'd talked to him, I could tell a difference, but I didn't know it was that bad. "I had no idea."

She sniffs. "Yeah, no one really does. It's so weird. He knew Rick and Travis today but didn't have a clue who I was. He was surprised that our foreman had hired a woman to work here."

She laughs like it's funny, but I can hear the pain in her voice. "Shit," I answer. "I'm sorry, honey. I'm going to come over tomorrow and see him."

"He'd like that. Thanks, Cole. I have to go. I have a few things I have to do before I can go to bed tonight."

I try not to let the image of Sassy laid back on a bed fill my thoughts, but that's exactly where my mind goes. Guilt hits me in the chest for thinking about her that way and knowing I shouldn't. "Okay, honey."

She's quiet, and normally I'd hang up but I'm waiting for her.

Her voice is soft. "I didn't know you had my number."

I clear my throat. "Yeah, I saved it a long time ago. And now you've got mine. Call me if you need anything. I'll see you tomorrow."

I hang up the phone before I do something crazy and reckless... like tell her how I feel about her.

# SASSY

It was a late night last night. By the time I finally made it to bed, I was exhausted, but sleep alluded me. All I could think about was that strange phone call from my neighbor, Cole Rogers. If I remember right, I think he's thirty-five, so he's around fourteen years older than me. He's a good man. At least he is to us. I've heard gossip in town on how he can be an asshole and hard to work for, but he's always been great to my dad and me. I'm sure at this point he's looking at us as a charity case or something. It's obvious to anyone that pays attention that we're losing control over here. I'm keeping the animals fed, but that's about it. It seems every day something else breaks.

I wish I could have stayed in bed this morning, but I knew I had a hundred things to do today, and first thing up is mucking some stalls. It's my least favorite chore, so I always do it first to get it out of the way.

"Hey, honey, how's it going this morning?"

I look over the top of the stall to see my dad with a cup of coffee in his hand. With a measured glance, I answer him, "Hey, uh, Amos. It's going good. How you doing this morning?"

I want to ask him if he knows my name, what year it is and a hundred other questions, but I don't. It seems the more I ask him sometimes the more frustrated he gets, so I'm determined to keep it light and simple. That's also why I call him Amos. I called him Dad one day, and he freaked out about it because he said he wasn't my dad. Yeah, I definitely don't want to do that again. I keep working and try to act as if everything is normal. Not as if I'm holding my breath, wondering if he knows I'm his daughter or not.

He glances around the barn and back at me. "We on a first-name basis now or what? I'm Dad, and it's good. I got a cup of coffee, got to see the sun rise, and get to work with my daughter side by side on our ranch.

Heck, honey, I don't think life can get any better than what it is right now."

I try to hold in my emotion. It seems anything can set him off sometimes, and I want to keep him like this for as long as I can. "I think you're right, Daddy. I can't think of anything either."

In the past, I would have been able to talk to him about the financial problems with the ranch, but I can't now. I can't even bring it up. The doctors tell me to treat him the same as I always have, but they were wrong because in the past, he could figure things out and make it better. Now it's like he can't wrap his head around the fact that we are slowly losing the ranch, and he can't figure out how to change it.

I lean against the pitchfork in my hand and smile at my dad. "Why don't you go porch sit for a while, Dad? I got everything taken care of here. I think Cole said he was going to come see you today."

He's nodding his head, and a big smile forms on his face when I mention Cole. "Sounds good. I'll do that."

He starts to walk away, and I can't take my eyes off him. He gets to the door before he turns around. "You like ranching, Sassy?"

The truth is, I don't know anything else. But I know what he wants to hear, so I say it. "I love it."

He smiles again. "That's good, honey, because I don't know what I'd do without the ranch."

My smile falters for just a second and then I force it back onto my face. As soon as he's out the door, I feel the pressure of it all on my shoulders, and I physically slump over. The weight is too much to bear, and I know I need to fix it. I have to. I can't let him lose his ranch. I won't.

I work through the morning. After I go inside to make sure my dad eats lunch, he takes a nap, and I find my way to the office at the front of our house. I pick up the documents that I received in the mail last week and read over them again. There's no point really. I've read them at least twenty times, and it still says the same thing. Even though it's a lot of words, it's pretty simple. If I join the Breeding Bidders Auction, I will be auctioning off my virginity. I get to keep one million dollars. And there is an option that includes marriage.

I found the site a few weeks ago when I was searching online on how to make some money. It's amazing all the sites I found that were get rich quick schemes, but this seems to be legit. I've had a phone conference with the owner and auctioneer, Coco St. James. She was snarky but at least answered all my questions. There's also a private auction coming up next week in Jasper, which is only thirty minutes away from me here in Whiskey Run. The deadline to apply is closing in, and I know I have to make a decision.

I've tried all I know to try. I've gone to the bank and asked for loans, I've sold off all I know to sell. I'm literally at the end of my rope. I have to do something or else I'm going to be looking for an apartment for me and my dad to live in.

And that will kill him. Literally, it will kill him if he isn't living on this ranch. I know it.

I shuffle things around on my desk, and when I find the pen, I grab it and count to ten. My mind is going crazy. All the things that could go wrong, all the risks in doing something like this, all of it is a lot to think about, but probably what's craziest is that my mind keeps going to Cole. I know it's stupid, but I've always secretly crushed on him. I know there's not a chance in hell with him so I shouldn't even be thinking about it, but I can't make myself stop. If I do this, if I give my virginity to some stranger, that's it. I won't be saving myself for Cole anymore.

I roll my eyes in disgust. I'm so stupid and need to get my head out of the clouds. Cole and I are never going to happen no matter how much I want him. He's a millionaire with one of the biggest ranches in Tennessee. He could literally have any woman he wanted. He's definitely not going to want some young tomboy whose ranch is falling down around her. Nope. It's best to get my head out of the clouds and start making things happen. The days of my dad saving the day are over. It's my turn now.

I lean over my desk and sign my name across the dotted line. Before I can talk myself out of it, I scan the page with my phone, open the email app, and send it in.

My phone makes the sound that it was sent, and I sigh loudly. It's done. No going back and forth anymore. The decision has been made.

My phone dings, and it's an email from Coco St. James. "I've been waiting for your email. See you soon."

I bite my lip. Doubt starts to creep in, but I shake it off. I can't lose this ranch, and this is the only option I have left to keep it. I'm doing what I have to do.

# COLE

I planned to go to the Reid Ranch early this morning, but one thing after another came up. By the time I make it over here, it's in the evening, and all the lights are off at the barn. I pull up to the small house, and even in the dark I can tell the porch needs repaired, shutters need replaced, and the house needs a new coat of paint. My hands flex around the steering wheel knowing that Sassy is living like this. She deserves so much more.

I push my way out of the truck and take my time up the steps. The screen door has holes in it and seems to be barely hanging on. I rap my knuckles on the door in three hard knocks and stand back.

I hear footsteps inside, and when the door opens, it's like a sucker punch to the gut. Sassy is standing before me in shorts and a T-shirt. Her long hair is piled in some kind of knot on the top of her head, and she's looking up at me with big green eyes. She's so beautiful she about takes my breath away. "Cole..."

Her voice is breathless as she leans against the door. "Dad's not here. His friend took him into town for some ice cream."

I'm holding the screen door open with my boot, and I shove my hands into the front pocket of my jeans. It's either that or reach for her. "Can I come in?"

She looks behind her and then back at me. At first I think she may have someone inside, but she steps back and opens the door wider to let me in. "Sure, uh, come on in."

I take my hat off my head and hold it as I walk in. She points to a hat rack, and I hang it on the hook before turning back to her. "So..."

She crosses her arms over her chest, and I try not to let my gaze go there. "So..." she mimics me. "What's going on?"

I point to a torn leather chair that I know is the one Amos usually sits in. "Can I sit down?"

She nods almost nervously, and her cheeks turn red. "Sure, have a seat."

I stand, waiting for her to sit. She finally moves to the couch and sits down, pulling her feet up under her.

I settle into the chair and lean forward, my elbows on my knees. "Tell me what's going on here at the ranch, Sassy."

Any friendliness on her face disappears in an instant. "We're not selling it, Cole."

I hold my hands up. I had stupidly made the mistake in the past of offering to buy the ranch from Amos. I think he stopped talking to me for at least six months after that. "I'm not offering to buy it. Regardless of what people think of me, I'm not a complete ass. I'm not trying to run you off your ranch. I want to help."

She's staring at me, her head tilted. I swear sometimes when she looks at me, she sees the real me. Not the millionaire rancher or the too bossy cowboy. I always feel that I can be myself around her, and it's a little unsettling.

She blinks twice and bites her lip. "I don't think that."

I shake my head in confusion. Obviously I can't even think around her because I can't keep up with a simple conversation. "You don't think what?"

She's not looking at me now. She's fiddling with her fingers, staring down at her hands. "I don't think you're an ass... I mean, I know you're not. You've always been good to Dad and to me."

Speechless, I want to move closer to her. I want to sit next to her on the couch, pull her into my arms, and make her forget all her worries.

She finally lifts her eyes to meet mine, and I smile at her. "Thank you, Sassy."

She shrugs as if it's not a big deal, but I know it is. "So how can I help?"

She holds up her hand. "You help us way more than you should already, Cole. You send over Travis and Rick, and I know you need them on your own ranch. You've helped us when the well pump went out, you helped us get the loan for the tractor a few years ago. You help us all the time."

I shrug because all of that is a drop in the bucket to me. "It's really not a big deal. I know that Amos won't like it, but maybe you and I can work something out. No one will have to know. I'll give you the money to fix what needs fixed around here, and we'll go from there."

Her mouth drops, and she closes it quickly. "I can't... I mean, I wish I could, but it's too late."

I watch her warily and see that she's on edge again. "What do you mean it's too late?"

She won't look at me. "Nothing. I didn't mean anything. Look, I can't take any handouts. I know this place needs work, but I've got it figured out and I'm going to fix it."

She's hiding something. It's obvious there's more going on here than I know about. I shouldn't have stayed away. Hell, it didn't help control my desire for her so it didn't help anyway. I don't know how else to do it but be blunt. "I'm worried about you."

"I'm fine. We're all fine. The ranch is fine-"

She doesn't get to finish because her phone starts to ring. She gets up and grabs it off the counter. She huffs as she answers. "Yeah?"

All I can hear is her side of the conversation. "I'll be right there."

She's stuffing her feet into boots as she hangs up the phone. "I have to go out to the barn. Prancer is trying to bust out of his stall."

"What? Frank can't handle an ornery horse?"

She walks to the door. "Frank won't deal with Prancer since he bit him a month ago. I need to go settle him down. You leaving? Staying...?"

"You want me to go to the barn with you?"

She laughs. "I think I can handle it."

I knew that's what she'd say, so I stay seated. "I'm going to hang out here. We have a few things to hash out."

She rolls her eyes and lets the door slam behind her on the way out. As soon as she's gone, I pull out my phone and open the notes app. I start making notes. *Porch, roof, paint inside.* I look at the yellow stain on the ceiling and add *roof leak.* I walk room to room making notes of things to get fixed. Sassy may not want my help, but I can't just stand idly by and let their house fall down around them. When I get to the office, I see the stack of papers on the desk. I know I shouldn't. I know it's a complete intrusion of their privacy, but I can't help it... especially after seeing the heading. Breeding Bidders Auction House Contract.

I read the page and notice Sassy's signature at the bottom. I stumble on my own feet. Everything is happening at once. I can literally hear the blood rushing to my head and something like a train whistle sounds in my ear. Woozy and dizzy, I lean against the desk to hold myself up. I hear the front door open, and I go to the office doorway.

Sassy is smiling until she sees my face and the paper I'm holding in my hand. I hold it up. "What the fuck is this?"

She reaches for the paper, but I pull it from her reach. "Answer me, Sassy. What is this?"

She doesn't like my tone, and I'm not aware enough to give a fuck right now. "It's none of your business, Cole. Why are you snooping anyway?"

I'm caught off guard when she lunges, pulling the paper from my hands. She folds it up and stuffs it in the pocket of her shorts. "I told you I'm taking care of things around here, and that's exactly what I'm doing."

# SASSY

I should probably be ashamed, but I'm not. I'm not doing the auction for some random reason. I'm doing it to save the ranch that's been in my family for generations. I'm doing it so my father doesn't lose the one thing he loves more than anything.

But I can tell that Cole doesn't see it that way. I've heard he has a temper, but I've never seen it before. Right now, he looks as if he's going to spontaneously combust. But I'm not scared. I know he would never hurt me, although he may yell a little.

His voice gets even louder. "Taking care of things? You call this taking care of things? You're auctioning off your body to God knows who. Do you have any idea what kind of man..."

I hold my hand up to stop him. I'm trying to remain calm and act as if I have complete control of the situation even though the thought of all of it still makes me nervous. "I know, Cole. I know exactly what can happen... just like I know what will happen if I don't do it. I can't let my father lose his ranch. I didn't know he took another mortgage out a few years ago. We're behind on payments, and we're going to lose this place. I've done everything I can. I've sold everything I have to sell, and this... me... is all there is left. Now if you're going to sit here and pass judgment on me, then just go. I don't need to hear it."

He moves toward me and puts his hands on my shoulders. I feel his touch as if it's a bolt of lightning that courses through my whole body. I try to remain calm even though just being this close to him has my nipples hard and my legs trembling. "Sassy, honey, you don't have to do this."

I bite my lip. If Cole had come last week to talk to me, would I have signed the paper? Probably. Because I know that deep down the only reason he is offering his help is because of how he feels about my family. He really is a good man. But I can't let him help me. I'll be in his debt forever, and eventually, one day, he's going to marry and have kids. I can't tie myself to him and watch all that from the sidelines. It will kill me.

With a calm and steady voice, I answer, "I can do this and I will. I've done it. I signed the contract and sent it in. I'm obligated now."

His hands tighten and trail down my arms to hold my hands. I look at where he's holding me and wish this was under different circumstances. His voice is gruff. "Bullshit. You can get out of it. I can get you out of it."

I shake my head vehemently. "No. There's a whole clause about it, and I'll owe money I don't have. It's done, Cole. It's happening."

"Fuck that. If you think I'm going to stand by and let you-"

I pull from his hold and step away from him. "Let me? You're going to let me... Cole, I understand that this is a little out of the ordinary, but you have no say on what I do. I know for some reason you think you need to take care of my dad-"

He grunts in frustration and slides his hand through his hair. His eyes are wild, and he's staring at me as if he's a caged animal or something. "Your dad? You think I'm doing this because of your dad? I'm doing it for you. I can't let... I can't stand by and watch you do this, Sassy. I can't."

I shrug my shoulders because obviously we're at a standstill. Neither one of us is going to give in, but he's about to find out I'm more stubborn than he thought.

He walks over to me, and I force myself to stay where I'm at. I refuse to show any weaknesses, and with Cole, I have them. Hell, he is my weakness. He reaches up and puts his palm against the side of my face. It takes everything in me to not lean into his touch. "Sassy... honey... what am I going to do with you?"

He's not expecting an answer. He's watching me so closely and with so much intent in his eyes, I couldn't even guess what's going to come out of his mouth next.

He brings his hand forward a little bit and slides his thumb across my bottom lip. I gasp because this is probably the most intimately I've ever been touched, and I want more. I stare up at him, not experienced enough to hide what I'm feeling. There's no doubt he can see my every thought right now.

"Have you ever been kissed before?"

I wasn't expecting that question, but I nod with just a small shake of my head. I don't want to move too much and risk him pulling away from me.

His thumb stops suddenly, and I whimper, hoping he doesn't take it away. "Who? Who kissed you?"

I should be embarrassed that I'm twenty-one years old and have almost no experience, but I'm not. I tell him truthfully, "Bobby James in second grade kissed me on the playground."

He swallows and nods his head. His thumb slides to the side of my mouth, and then he grips my chin softly. "Is that it? That was your only kiss?"

I nod and blink up at him. It's almost as if I'm in a trance, wondering what's going to happen next.

His nostrils flare, and he leans closer to me. "I'm going to kiss you, Sassy."

I barely comprehend what he's saying before he dips his head and presses his lips to mine. It's a small kiss, just a peck, but when he pulls back, I reach up and wrap my hand around the nape of his neck. If this is the only chance I'll ever get to kiss him, I want a real one. "I wasn't ready. Kiss me again, Cole."

He doesn't have to be told twice. He smiles before leaning down and kissing me again. His lips mesh with mine, and he tilts his head to press harder into me. He lifts just slightly. "Open your mouth, honey. Let me in."

This time when he kisses me, I open my mouth just slightly, and I'm not ready for the way his tongue sweeps in, sliding against my own. I whimper as he kisses me, melding our lips together. My whole body comes alive as he pulls me into his body. I may be shorter than him, but somehow we fit together perfectly. His hands slide down my back and rest on the top of my ass. I press my body against his, wanting to feel the hard strength of him, but I'm not prepared for the growing bulge that is pressing into my belly. I pull back, breathless. His lips are swollen, and I know mine are the same. I shouldn't look, I know I shouldn't, but I lower my gaze until I'm staring at his hard manhood pressed against the front of his jeans. He's hard...

"Is that... is that because of me?"

He reaches down and adjusts himself. "Yeah, honey, that's definitely because of you."

I stand here in awe wondering what alternate universe I'm in. I can't help but keep watching the bulge between his legs, and I swear it twitches as I'm watching it.

He takes a step toward me. "Is that so hard to believe? I'm aroused by you, Sassy."

My eyes about pop out of my head. I know he's not saying he loves me or anything like that, but just the idea that me, tomboy Sassy Reid, has done this to Cole Rogers is crazy. I'm speechless, and he takes another step toward me. "Just like you're aroused by me."

He reaches out and puts one finger to my chest. I suck in a breath as his finger traces around my hard, puckered nipple.

My whole body shudders as he plucks it between his thumb and forefinger. I reach out and grab on to his upper arms to steady myself. My legs feel like jelly and like they might buckle at any minute.

He just smiles. His voice is thick. "You like that, don't you?"

I nod my head as he continues touching and caressing me. "Do you want to lose your virginity to just anyone, Sassy?"

His words are like a bucket of ice water thrown in my face. I pull away from him and hide my traitorous body behind a blanket that was lying on the back of the couch. "Is that what this is, Cole? A test? You need to prove that I'll open my legs for just anyone?"

"What? No, of course not. I want you to understand what you're getting into."

I blow out a breath and march to my front door, yanking it open. "I know exactly what I'm getting myself into, but thanks for the lesson, Cole. You can leave now."

"Sassy." His voice is like a warning, but I'm not giving in.

I point outside into the darkness. "Go, Cole. Please, I just want to be left alone. Thank you for what you've done for my family, but you've done enough."

He wants to argue. I can see on his face that he doesn't want to go, but I'm not giving in. I've made my choice, and even if it's not the right one, it's what has to be done.

He walks toward me and stops at the door. He grabs his hat and leans down, forcing me to look at him. "This isn't over, Sassy. And just so you know, that...

what we shared.... that's not normal... it's not usually like that... It won't feel like that with someone else."

With those words, he walks out the door, calling over his shoulder, "I'll be seeing you soon."

Instead of standing on the porch and watching him until he drives away like I normally would, I slam the door behind him.

So many emotions are going through my head, and I let them take over until I'm in a crying heap in my bed. This... all of it... was just a game to him. I've dreamed of kissing him, and now I'll never get the feeling of it actually happening out of my mind. It may have been some kind of stupid lesson for him... but to me it was everything.

# COLE

I fucked up. I know I did.

I wasn't kissing her to teach her some kind of fuckin' lesson. I kissed her because I wanted to, because I needed to. Just the thought of her with another man has me wanting to kill someone.

I barely slept last night and rode out onto my ranch just as the sun was coming up. I know I need to think and figure out things, and the best place for me to do it is on the back of a horse. I ride until my horse Zeus and I are both breathless. I didn't have a plan on where I was going, but it's not completely strange that I end up out at the old swimming hole that's on the edge of the Reid property line. I sit on Zeus and stare at the big magnolia tree, remembering the past.

It was shortly after Sassy had turned twenty last year that I found her out here in nothing but her bra and panties, swimming.

My cock flexes in my jeans just remembering the way she looked as she climbed out of the water.

I stare at the exact spot I saw her and get lost back in time. It was only last year, but it could have been yesterday it's so vivid in my mind.

*She doesn't realize I'm watching her. My horse is grazing at the grass beneath his feet and I'm gripping the leather reins in my hand tightly.*

*She's smiling, not a care in the world. She doesn't realize that her underwear is translucent and is showing everything. Either that or she doesn't care because she thinks she's out here alone.*

*"Sassy," I say, and my voice falters with a squeak. I clear my throat and try again. "Sassy," I say louder.*

*Her head jerks as she finally spots me. I climb off of my horse and tie him to the fence before jumping over it onto her land. She's watching me, smiling.*

*I take her in from the top of her head to the ends of her bare toes. She's curvy, and she's definitely a woman now.*

"Hey, Cole," she says with a smile on her face.

I pull my hat lower on my head as if that's going to stop her from seeing the attraction on my face. "Sassy, you shouldn't be out here."

She looks at the fence line and back at me in confusion. "I shouldn't be out on my property?"

"You're at least two miles from your house, and no one's around."

She points to her horse that's tied up to the tree. She has a rifle hooked into her saddle bag. Rolling her eyes, she tells me, "I have my rifle. I'm protected, Cole."

Stubbornly, I tell her, "You still shouldn't be out here...in your underwear."

It's then that she realizes what she's wearing. She looks down at herself and sure enough, she spots her hard nipples pointing right at me through her thin bra. Her face turns red, but she doesn't try to hide herself. Nope, she wouldn't be Sassy if she did. If anything, she pulls her shoulders back, pushing her breasts out even more. "I don't see what the big deal is. I was out here by myself."

I walk closer to her, and she wavers for just a minute. I think she's going to take a step back, but she surprises me when she stays where she's at. I walk around her because

*I'm an idiot and a glutton for punishment, wanting to see all of her. Her ass is perfect globes, and my hands are itching to grab on to them.*

*I move back around to the front of her.* "You're not here by yourself now. Anyone could walk up on you."

*She lifts her head and boldly meets my gaze.* "Yeah, but it's just you, Cole. I'm not afraid of you."

*My eyes glitter. I want to bend her over my knee and spank her pretty ass for putting herself in this position. It's probably true that no one would stumble on her out here, but if I did, one of my ranch hands or her dad's ranch hands could do the same.*

"You shouldn't be afraid of me."

*She shrugs.* "I'm not."

*I smile and put my hands deep into my pockets.* "You walk around your ranch like that?"

*She looks down at herself as if she doesn't see what the big deal is. I swear this image of her is burned into my mind forever. I won't be forgetting it.* "In my underwear? No, of course not."

*I nod, and I know I shouldn't ask the next question, but I do it anyway. Maybe because it's just the two of us out here and it's the only time I've ever been completely alone with her. Or maybe because she's all I've thought about, and I need to know the answer. "Anyone see you like that? Ever?"*

*She scrunches her nose up and seems to think about it. "Are we counting the girls in gym class in high school?"*

*I shake my head side to side.*

*She brings out her hand and acts as if she's counting on her fingers. When she gets to her second hand, I'm ready to go off. But then she raises her head with a glint in her eye. "Just one person... just you."*

*I let out the breath that I didn't realize I was holding. It comes out in a big poof of air. "So I'm the only man to have seen you in your underwear?"*

*She swallows, licks her lips, and nods her head. "Yep."*

*It's not my place, and I know I should keep my damn mouth closed, but I can't hold it in. "That's good, Sassy. Boys your age only want one thing. You should wait... before you show another man what you look like under your clothes."*

*She leans down and looks at herself again. "What do you mean? I look the same with clothes on... or at least a bathing suit."*

*I shake my head and try to hide my laugh. She may be twenty years old, but her dad has sheltered her most of her life. I'm sure it doesn't help that I've made sure to keep men away from her. "No, honey. Trust me. You definitely look different like that."*

*She tilts her head to look at me. There's a question in her eyes, and before I change my mind, I say to her, "What is it? You look like you have a question. What is it?"*

*She licks her lips nervously. "I do have a question."*

*I nod, following the path that her tongue took across her lips. "Yeah, you can ask me."*

*She nods and swallows hard. "The boys at school always made fun of me. Said I was an ugly tomboy. Do you think I'm ugly? I mean, do you think any man will ever look at me and think I'm pretty?"*

*Two thoughts go through my head. The first is that teenage boys are idiots. The second is that I'm wondering how she doesn't see what I see.*

*I lift my hat off my head and hold it to my chest. "Okay, so whatever idiots said that to you lied. They probably said it because they knew they weren't good enough for you-"*

*She interrupts me with a surprised gasp. "Good enough for me?"*

*"Yes. You're pretty, Sassy. Smart, kind, funny, independent, you don't take shit from people, you're good with animals..." I let my voice trail off before I admit to her what I really think about her. About how she's always on my mind and I dream about her every night. Yeah, I'd better keep that to myself. "One day, you'll find a man that treats you right. Don't waste your time on the ones that don't see your value."*

*She nods her head, and a grin overtakes her face. "You think I'm pretty?"*

*I laugh. Of everything that I just said, that's what she's hung up on. "You're beautiful, Sassy. Don't let anyone ever make you think different. If they do, tell me and I'll take care of it."*

*She looks at me curiously. "Why are you being nice to me?"*

*I gape at her. "Aren't I always nice to you?"*

*She tilts her head back to look at me. "Yeah, you are, but you never talk to me."*

*I don't deny it. As a matter of fact, I go out of my way to avoid talking to her, but I can't explain why. "Will you do me a favor?"*

*She doesn't hesitate. She nods her head vigorously, always happy to please.*

*I put my hat back on my head and shove it down over my forehead. "Don't go showing your body to men that aren't worthy, sweetie. Promise me no more swimming in your underwear."*

*She shrugs. "Okay, I promise."*

I remember that I forced myself to walk away from her after that. I could have stayed and talked to her all day, but I knew I wouldn't be satisfied with just looking at her. No, I would have wanted to touch her, and I knew I shouldn't.

I turn Zeus around and look in the direction of Sassy's ranch. Can I let her do this? Can I let her auction herself off and maybe marry another man? All this time, she's been right next door and I've told myself that I'm too old for her and she deserves a better man than me, but we've reached a crossroads. I let her do this and I may lose her forever.

Fuck! I know I can't let her do it. I can't sit by and let another take what's mine—and Sassy's mine. She has been since the day I saw her coming out of the water in her underwear.

With determination, I ride back toward the ranch. I have a lot to do and not a lot of time to do it. First, I need to wrangle myself an invite to this auction... and then I'm going to win me a virgin.

# SASSY

I'm going to be sick.

This week has flown by, and the day has come for the auction. I'm having second thoughts. Hell, third and fourth too. Ever since that kiss that Cole laid on me the other night, I've been a mess. I know now I overreacted. So many times this week, I almost called him to apologize, but I didn't. I know Cole, and I know that he was just worried about me.

But it's too late now.

I'm backstage at the auction, and my whole life is about to change.

Most likely I won't be a virgin by the end of the night.

The thought makes me want to run out of here as fast as I can and not look back.

But then just as quickly, thoughts of my father and his beloved ranch surface. He's the reason I'm doing this. My mother died when I was just two years old, and my dad raised me by himself. He's sacrificed his whole life to give me everything I could want or need. I can do this for him.

My hands tremble as one of Coco St. James' assistants hands me a costume that is hidden in a hanging bag. "What's this?"

The woman rolls her eyes. "It's what you're wearing tonight. Coco picked it out, and I have to say, it's perfect."

She turns and walks across the room, grabs a cowboy hat, and brings it back to me. "Here you go. This will go perfectly with it."

I take the hat from her with a nod. I'm hoping there's a pair of jeans and a flannel shirt in the hanging bag, but I know it's not going to be the case. The other women are already dressed, and it looks like a competition to see who can wear the least amount of clothes.

I set the hat on the chair behind me and hang the bag on a hook to unzip it. I hold my breath as I unveil the outfit. The white material is no surprise. It looks like all the other women are wearing white tonight. It's a silky material, and as I lift it out, I open the bag to see where the rest of it is. I look over at the woman next to me, who's fixing her hair in the mirror. "I don't think I've ever worn anything this short in my life."

She laughs and holds up the garment. "Cute. It's going to look great."

I take it back from her with a doubtful look.

I strip down to my bra and panties and then put the outfit on. It's a short dress that looks like overalls on the top. I twist side to side, thinking this can't be right.

The woman next to me laughs again. "You can't wear a bra with that. Did you read the instructions? No bras for this auction."

I clench my eyes shut and shake my head. What was I thinking? Not only am I agreeing to have sex with some man I don't even know, I'm now going to have to parade my almost naked body in a room full of men.

I release the clasp of my bra and pull the straps down my arms and stuff it into my bag. I huff and start searching through the bag that held the outfit. Surely there's more to it. I put my hand on a piece of silk at the bottom of the bag and pull it out. Sure enough, it's the tiniest piece of underwear I've ever seen. I take off my own and put the scrap of material on. The string goes up my ass, and I shift uncomfortably. You have to be shitting me. Women actually choose to wear these things?

Panic starts to rise, and I sit down in the chair. I focus on a pair of white cowboy boots sitting under the garment bag and take deep breaths. I try to clear my mind, but it's not working. Because every thought I have is of Cole Rogers.

The woman next to me comes and puts her hand on my back. "We're almost up. Are you okay?"

I shake my head and keep breathing. "I don't think I can do this."

She tilts her head and stares at me with a measured look. She grabs my arms and helps me stand up. "Okay, tell me... sorry, what's your name?"

"Sassy. My name is Sassy."

She smiles and nods. "Right. Sassy, tell me, if you say fuck it and walk out the door, what will you lose?"

I stutter, "A million dollars."

She pins me with a look. "No, honey, that's just money. I'm talking about the reason you're here... or are you just here for the money?"

Finally, I get what she's asking. "I lose my family's ranch. The one that's been in my family for generations. If that happens, I'll probably lose my father because he won't make it if he has to leave his ranch. He would be devastated."

She nods, smiling. "Right. See, now we're getting somewhere. Okay, so say you leave here and lose your ranch, let your dad down... can you live with yourself?"

I choke back a sob. "No."

She nods excitedly. "Okay, so say you stay and go through with this. What do you lose?"

My first thought is of course Cole, but I don't mention him. It's not like he's mine to lose. So I say the one thing I know I'll lose. "My virginity."

She laughs. "Yep, and can you live with that?"

I know what she wants me to say. I'm not proud of what I'm doing, but I'm going to do it all the same. "Yeah, I can."

She leans over and grabs the white cowboy boots and squats down in front of me. "Lift."

I do as she says, and she helps me put my boots on. "Now get out there. You got this, Sassy!"

I impulsively reach for her. "Thank you."

She shrugs and pats me on the back. "It's nothing. Good luck."

I nod and walk over to the curtain to get in line. There are two women in front of me, and I pull my shoulders back. *I can do this. I can do this.*

I keep moving forward, repeating my little mantra and hoping that I'll start to believe it soon. Because whether I want to do this or not, I have to. I can't turn back now.

# COLE

I sit on the edge of my seat and look up at the lighted stage. This whole thing is insane, but I'm not leaving without Sassy. It took me a week to get the invitation to this thing. I've had all kinds of credit checks, background checks, and everything done, and now here I sit waiting for the announcer to say Sassy's name.

At least it's tasteful. I don't know what I was expecting, but I'm surprised. Everything is done in fine detail, and every security measure is in place. Limos, jets, and helicopters surround the place, and the inside of the grand white tent is impressive.

I got here early, wanting to make sure I didn't have any problems getting through security. It took a while, but

I can't complain about it because it seems they take their job of keeping the women safe seriously.

But I'm ready to get this over with. I'm not going to breathe easy until I have Sassy in my arms and we're on our way back to Whiskey Run.

The longer I sit here, the more on edge I become. I've watched woman after woman be auctioned off, and it fuckin' pains me to know that Sassy is going to be up there for other men to look at and bid on. They may bid, but they'll never win. I'll bet my whole damn ranch if I have to. Sassy is mine.

The woman with the blunt blond bob that gave her name as Coco St. James – what kind of name is that anyway? - is getting ready to announce the next person, and I know it's Sassy. Even before she says a word, I have goosebumps, and the hair on the back of my neck is standing up.

I move farther to the edge of my seat and put my hand on the bidding button. We were told that when we want to bid, all we need to do is push the button. As soon as Mrs. St. James says Sassy's name, I'm holding on to the button, not letting it go.

She introduces Sassy as a virgin cowgirl that knows how to ride. Fuck me, I can't sit here through this. I jump from my seat, still holding on to that damn button. Other chairs in the room are lighting up, and it pisses me off. They have the audience in the dark so I can't give the evil eye to anyone. All I can do is keep holding that button, determined to win my virgin.

The whole time, I keep my eyes trained on Sassy. She's not comfortable up there. No one else may notice, but I sure can tell. I'm ready for this to be over.

Coco St. James stops talking and presses her finger to her earpiece before announcing, "Bidder #75, you have to let go of the button. You're outbidding yourself."

I growl in frustration, and it fills the room. Sassy's head jerks up, and I wonder if she realizes it's me out here. Could she have recognized my voice?

Reluctantly, I take my finger off the button and hover over it instead. Mrs. St. James continues, "Sassy, you have the crowd excited. Okay, so bidding is at three million. Do I have three point two million?"

Another man bids, and I hit my button before she asks for another one. The bidding continues, and I'm determined to win. I don't care if I'm outbidding myself; I'm not leaving anything to chance. Finally, when it's reached six million and Mrs. St. James announces bidder #75 as the winner, I'm out of my seat and heading to the stage.

Sassy is being directed where to go, and I can see her trembling as she walks down the steps. A security guard tries to stop me, holding me back, and I say Sassy's name.

Her head jerks up. "Cole?" When she sees me, she says my name again and starts running to me.

I move to the side and catch her against my chest as her arms and legs wrap around me. I hold on to her, refusing to let go. I squeeze her hard because all I can think about is what would have happened if I wasn't here. Losing Sassy is not an option.

"You need to put her down until you've transferred the funds."

The security guard puts his hands on Sassy as if he's going to take her away from me. He doesn't have a clue how far I'll go to keep her in my arms. I hold on to her a little tighter. "Take your hands off her."

He looks into my eyes, and he must see how serious I am. He throws his hands up, palms facing me. "You have to pay, man. I'm just trying to do my job."

I nod in understanding. "I'll pay. But you'll keep your hands off her."

"Fine." The security guard gives up trying to hold me back and instead puts a hand to my back and leads me to the exit.

I carry Sassy with me, her face buried in my neck. For the first time in a week, I finally start to relax.

She's mine now.

I stop at the cashier and sign my name, approving the wire transfer. He points out the door. "If you want the marriage option, turn left. Forgoing it? You're free to go. Parking lot is to the right."

I nod and start walking with Sassy still in my arms.

This whole week, I convinced myself that I was going to win the auction, take her home, and be done with this nonsense. But my heart and my feet have a mind of their own. Instead of turning right to the parking lot, I turn to the left. I carry her up the hill to where another white smaller tent is set up. This wasn't the plan, and I don't know what is going to happen when we get home, but I know Sassy's going to be my wife.

# SASSY

I can't believe that Cole came and bid on me. Not only bid, but won me in the auction. I was so scared up on that stage. All I kept thinking about was that kiss I shared with Cole. I knew I was messing up, but I didn't know what to do.

When I stumbled down the stairs and heard him call my name, the emotions welled up inside me, and I've been in his arms ever since. I know I'm making a spectacle of myself, but I don't even care.

I keep my head buried in his neck, and it's as we're walking out of the building that I finally talk to him. "Thank you, Cole. You didn't have to do this, but I'm glad you're the one that won the auction. I'm going to pay you back."

I start to cry. I try to hold it back, but I can't. All the what-ifs are swarming in my head, and I can't seem to make heads or tails of any of it. All I know is that I've never been happier to see someone in my life than when I heard Cole say my name.

He doesn't say anything. He just grunts and keeps walking. I don't look to see where we're going. I don't even care.

It's not until he stops and goes to set me down that I hold on to him tighter. His voice is calm. "Let go, Sassy."

Reluctantly, I do as he asks. I unhook my legs from around his trim waist and slide down the length of his body. He grunts as my feet touch the floor. He's still holding me, one hand on my back, and the other touches my chin, lifting it so I have to look into his eyes. He frowns and starts to wipe at the tears on my cheeks. His voice breaks in a whisper. "What am I going to do with you, Sassy?"

I could think of a few things and start to name them off in my head. *Kiss me. Love me. Never let me go.* But of course, I don't say any of those things.

"Are you ready?"

A man comes to stand next to us, and he's looking between Cole and me. I drag my eyes off Cole and look at the man smiling at us as if he's in on some kind of secret.

Cole grabs my hand and turns to the man. "We're ready."

The man starts talking, and I know my eyes about bug out of my head. I turn to Cole and interrupt the man's spiel. "Are we getting married?"

Cole turns his head and levels me with a look. His face is guarded, and I have no way of knowing what he's thinking. "Yes, we're getting married."

I shake my head. He's already paid six million dollars to save me from this mess. I can't make him do this too.

"You don't have to-"

He cuts me off. "We're getting married, Sassy. I think that's the only way I'm going to be able to keep you out of trouble."

I don't know what I was expecting. Maybe hoping for something romantic like he can't live without me, but no, he's marrying me to keep me out of trouble. As if I'm some child or something. "You don't... I won't..." I start.

But he doesn't let me finish. "It's happening. When we leave here, you're going to be Mrs. Sassy Rogers."

I don't have any fight left in me. Have I dreamed about this moment? At least a hundred times... but I never wanted it like this.

I close my mouth and look at the man in front of us. He gives me a look of pity. "You ready to do this, miss?"

I nod my head and think about how ridiculous this all is. I'm listening to the man talk about commitment and forever, and I'm standing here in a see-through nightie. I chance a glance over at Cole, and his jaw is pulled tight. He doesn't look as if he's a man that's happy about getting married.

When it's time, Cole answers the officiant, "I do."

His voice is clear and calm. Nothing like what I'm feeling. But when it's my turn, I nod my head. "I do."

The officiant smiles, announces us as husband and wife, and tells Cole he can kiss the bride.

I turn to face him, and Cole is not happy. If anything, he looks pissed. I wait for him to refuse to kiss me, but he surprises me when he pulls me into his arms. He leans down until our mouths are only inches apart. He pauses, and I search his eyes, trying to get a glimpse of what he's thinking. He didn't have to marry me. This was just an added option that he could have refused, but for some reason, he didn't.

He looks as if he's about to pull away, and I grab the lapels of his suit jacket. "Kiss me, Cole."

He nods and slowly leans in to press his lips to mine. I loop my arms around his neck and hold on. His kiss is potent, and he pulls me against his body, letting me feel his hard body against my softer one. I don't want to let him go. If I had my choice, I'd stay right here because it's like all my fantasies are coming true.

Cole pulls away first, and we're both breathless. He looks down at me, his eyes traveling down my body. He stares at my hard nipples poking against the sheer material of my white overalls. He grunts as he takes off his jacket and wraps it around me. I slide my arms inside it and am instantly comforted, surrounded by the heat and scent of his body.

He turns to the officiant. "Where do we sign?"

He's holding out a marriage license, and both Cole and I sign it. It isn't long before we're both settled in his truck and headed back to Whiskey Run.

There's a thousand questions in my head, but each time I think I get the nerve up to ask him one, I look at him, and his jaw is tight, and he's frowning at the road in front of us.

I hold my hands in my lap and stare out the window at the scenery passing by. There's peace in knowing that I'm going to be able to save my dad's ranch but at what cost? This changes everything.

I have no idea what is going to happen now. But when Cole passes the driveway to his ranch and takes the one to mine, I know that even though he bought me and even married me, it looks as if I'm going to remain a virgin.

I sigh, unable to keep in my disappointment.

# COLE

My truck rocks across the gravel driveway. All the way home to Whiskey Run, I've held on to the steering wheel with a death grip. It was either that or reach for Sassy.

I've been hard and pissed off the whole time, and it's not a good situation to be in. I've never been the type of person to be out of control or impulsive, but obviously if it involves Sassy, I'll do just about anything. Even get married.

She's been silent the whole way, but her soft voice fills the cab of the truck as we arrive at her house. "You're mad at me."

I ignore her. I don't trust myself to say the right things, so maybe it's better if I say nothing at all.

The lights are off at her barn and her house. I'm sure her father's already in bed, so I turn off my lights as I park.

She starts to get out, and I tell her to stay.

Thinking she'll listen, I get out of my side of the truck and walk around to find her shutting her door.

"I thought I told you to-"

"Stay? You did. But I'm not a dog. I don't know why you're mad at me. I didn't ask you to come and bid on me.... to marry me."

I take a step toward her. She still has my jacket on, but it does nothing to hide her heaving breasts from the little tirade she just had.

"Did you really think I'd just leave you there?"

She sort of deflates right in front of me. She puts her head in her hand, and I watch as she seems to gather her thoughts. She looks up at me. "Cole, listen, if I could go back, I would have just taken the money you offered me. Instead you're out six million dollars, and you're married to someone you don't want to be married to. I know I messed up, but I'm going to pay you back. Somehow, some way, I'm going to pay you back every last penny. I just can't stand you being mad at me."

I pull her out from the front of the truck door and open it before setting her up in the seat. She's turned to the side, her feet on the step and her knees out. I fit my body between her legs and lift her chin to look at me. "I don't care about the money, Sassy. I care about you. I'd pay that over and over to make sure you're okay."

She leans forward. "Then why are you mad?"

I let out a deep breath and search her eyes in the moonlight. She has no clue. I lean forward and press my forehead to hers as I take big, deep, calming breaths. I have to keep reminding myself that she's safe.

Finally when I feel I have some semblance of control, I lift my head. "I'm mad because anything could have happened tonight, Sassy. I know you wanted to save this ranch for your dad. I get that, I really do. But what about you?"

She shakes her head. "What do you mean?"

I blow out a breath. Does she really not know her worth? "I mean what about you? What if you were bought by someone that drank too much, that beat you, that hurt you? What if they wanted to take you away from here... away from me?"

She puts her stubborn nose in the air. "I didn't have an option."

I grunt. "As long as there is a breath in me, you have an option. I'm your option from now on, Sassy. Anytime you're scared, worried, whatever. I'm your option."

And because I can't hold back anymore and she makes me want to lose control, I lean in to kiss her. She opens her mouth, and I slide my tongue along hers. I deepen the kiss, and it turns into a desperate mashing of our mouths together. All the emotions I've felt this evening I'm putting into the mating of our lips. I could have lost her tonight.

She whimpers, and I pull away, afraid I'm hurting her.

She reaches to hold me close. "No, please don't stop."

I put my hand on her chest and push her back on the seat. She lies down, propped up on her elbows, looking at me. My jacket that she's wearing has fallen open, and her nipples are hard under the night's cool air. Her white nightgown that barely covered her ass has risen up to her waist. Fuck, I know I shouldn't, but I can't stop. I slide my hand from her chest, down her stomach and to the apex of her thighs. I touch her through the silk material and find that she's soaked.

I push the barely there material to the side and slide my finger through her wet slit. When I brush over her clit, she groans. My voice is gruff. "You don't get it, Sassy. If I wasn't there, someone else would be touching you like this right now."

I circle her clit, and her hips start to lift up and down. "Some other man would be touching you, pleasing you, thinking that you were theirs."

Already she's so close. I apply more pressure. "Do you hear what I'm saying, Sassy? Another man... fuck, I don't even want to think about it. That's why I'm mad. I could have lost you tonight. You could have had another man's last name, and I couldn't let that happen. You're mine now, honey. Mine."

I bend over and press my tongue to her throbbing clit. Her taste hits my tongue, and I devour her. I'm relentless as I give her pleasure. Her hand goes to the back of my head, and she holds me there one second and then starts pulling my hair the next. She's so close, and I won't stop until she explodes on my tongue.

I slide a finger inside her just to my knuckle and push in and out. Her body tenses, and all at once, her hips lift, and she starts to writhe underneath me. She grunts and groans, and the whole time, I keep my mouth on her clit with my finger pumping inside her. Her body rolls with the orgasm, and I lap at her, savoring the taste.

When she falls limp against the seat of my truck, I kiss her mound one more time and then stand up. She's primed, and it would take nothing for me to pull my hard cock out and take her. She wouldn't stop me.

But this is not the way I want things to happen. She's been through enough shit today, and I need her head right for when I do finally take her. I need it to be her choice... not because of some auction or a feeling that she owes me. I've taken enough from her tonight.

I help her out of the truck, and when she stands on her two feet, her legs about buckle.

I swing her up into my arms and carry her up onto the porch. I reach for the front door, and it's unlocked. I don't dare carry her across the threshold. No, I need to put some distance between us.

"Goodnight, Sassy. Lock this door."

She shakes her head in confusion. "But..."

"I'll see you soon," I tell her before forcing myself to turn and walk away. With her taste still on my tongue, it's the hardest thing I've ever had to do.

# SASSY

The last two days have been busy. I've been getting everything lined out. I went to the bank and paid off the mortgage my dad had taken out. I paid off the balance I owed at the feedlot, I hired a crew to start on the barn's roof next week, and I went into Jasper and bought a herd of cows, hired another ranch hand, and found a nurse for my father.

I tried to make sure I only spent the money on the things we had to have, but I did splurge while I was in town and bought myself a new pair of jeans, blouse, and even a dress. The whole time, I've had my phone glued to my hand. I've been waiting to hear something – anything – from Cole, and by the morning of the third day, I know I need to go and talk to him.

I put on my new jeans and a V-neck T-shirt. I apply some mascara and lip gloss and then brush my hair until it shines. The whole way over to his house, I have to fan myself, wondering how it's going to be when I look into his face. I know I'm not going to be able to look at him without thinking about what he did to me the other night. That seems to be all I've thought about.

I pull into his driveway and spot his truck sitting next to the barn. I pull in next to it and get out. Every time I'm here, it takes my breath away. His ranch is what dreams are made of. I barely get a few steps out of the truck and I see Cole walking out of the barn. His walk is self-assured and confident. He's got his dark denim jeans on, and his hat is low on his head. I take in the way he has his shirt rolled up to his elbows, showing off his muscled forearms. Already, my heart is starting to race, and he's like 15 feet from me.

"Hey, Cole."

He stops suddenly and turns to me. He doesn't smile or even acknowledge me, and my nerves settle in. I go around his truck and stop a few feet from him. "Do you have time to talk?"

He nods but still doesn't move.

Nervously, my hands fidget together. "Okay, uh, well I wanted to tell you that I got things lined out with what had to be paid. I wanted to give you back what was left, and I hoped maybe we can talk about a payment plan or something."

I can't read his expression, but his voice tells me that there's no arguing with him about this. "You're not paying me back."

I put my hand on my hip. "I have to."

He shakes his head. "We're not talking about this, Sassy. Forget it. We don't ever have to talk about it again."

My heart stutters in my chest. What does he mean we don't ever have to talk about it again? Is it the money he's talking about or all of it? I mean, we're married. We didn't have to be; that was his choice, but it still remains that we're married. "So we're not going to talk about what exactly, Cole? The money, the other night, the fact that we're married? Or have you already forgotten?"

He takes a step toward me and then stops suddenly. His hands are in fists at his sides. "The money. We're not going to talk about the money. I haven't forgotten that we're married, and I sure as fuck haven't forgot about what happened when you came on my tongue the other night."

I can feel the heat rise in my face, but I push forward. "Right. So are we going to talk about it?"

Before he can answer me, Cole's foreman, Jake, comes out of the barn. "Boss, wait a minute-"

He cuts off when he spots me standing here. He eyes me from the top of my newly cut hair to my boots and then back up again. "Sassy, is that you? Well, aren't you a sight. You sure have grown up."

I lock my hands behind my back. I'm always nervous when people compliment me. I guess it's because I'm not used to it. "Thank you."

He nods and starts walking toward me. For the first time since Cole saw me, he starts to move. He positions himself between Jake and me. "What do you need, Jake?"

Even though Cole sounds rude, it doesn't faze Jake. "The feedlot called. Their delivery truck is broke down in Jasper, so I'm going to town to get our order. You need anything while I'm there?"

Cole shakes his head. "No, I can't think of anything."

Jake nods and looks past Cole to me. "What about you, Sassy? Need anything? I can drop it off at your ranch on my way back through."

I shake my head. "No, I think we're good."

He nods, smiling. "How's your dad?" Before I can answer, he continues, "I haven't seen him in a long time. I should come over and see him. Maybe I can take you out to dinner or something afterward."

I know I look like a fish as my mouth opens, closes, and opens again. Speechless, I'm about to stutter something when Cole holds his hand out. "You can shut that shit down right now."

Jake starts to laugh and pats Cole on the shoulder. "It's all right there, big brother. I'll have her home by midnight."

Jake goes to take a step toward me, and Cole moves in front of him. "I'm not her brother, and you won't be taking her out."

They both are tense, staring at one another. I've never in my life been in a situation like this so I just stand here, not knowing what to say. All I do know is that Cole is pissed. I reach for him, putting a hand to his back. He turns and looks over his shoulder at me. He glares as if he's pissed off at the world, but when he sees my crestfallen face, his features soften.

# COLE

I don't want to scare Sassy. It's obvious she doesn't know what to think with Jake and me squared off against one another. I try to smile at her, but I'm sure I look more like I'm grimacing than anything.

But there's no way I'm going to stand by and let him think he has a chance with Sassy because he doesn't. Not a chance in hell.

I take a step toward Sassy and thank God she doesn't back away. I put one arm over her shoulder and glare at Jake. "You won't be taking her out, Jake, and I'll tell you why. You're asking to take my wife out on a date, and you should know me well enough to know that I don't share."

Jake and Sassy both gasp. I'm sure I've surprised Sassy. We haven't talked about the marriage or anything, but I'm sure she didn't expect me to announce it to anyone either. I'm a little surprised myself, but there's no way I'm going to let people think that she's free because she's not. She's mine.

Jake looks between Sassy and me. "Are you sure you're married? Because Sassy even looks surprised."

Fuck, I should have just punched his ass and been done with it. He may be my foreman, but I don't put up with shit from anyone. "Yes, she knows we're married, and I know if I catch you looking at my wife again like you did a minute ago that you'll be looking for another job."

Sassy turns in my arms and puts her hand on my waist. "Cole, don't..."

I look down at her. "Sorry, honey, that's the way it is. Before he didn't know, so I'm giving him a pass. But now he does, and if he looks at you or even thinks of asking to spend time with you, then he'll be buried six feet under on this ranch somewhere."

Her eyes widen, and she blinks up at me. I force my gaze away from her and give a challenging look to Jake. "Are we clear, Jake?"

Jake's not happy about it, and I can't say I blame him. But it is what it is. He holds his hands up. "Yeah, sure, man, we're clear. Congratulations, I guess. I'm going to head into town."

I nod and watch him walk away. Sassy is still standing under my arm, her hand on my waist, and I release her. She groans and puts her head in her hands. "The whole town will know we're married by this evening, Cole."

I shrug my shoulders. "So what?"

She shakes her head, and by the look on her face, I know what she's going to say. I hold my hand up. "Think about it, Sass. If you're about to say anything to me about money, stop now. I don't want to hear it."

"No, it's not that. I'm just confused, that's all."

I cross my arms over my chest. "Confused about what?"

"You obviously don't want to be married to me."

My arms tighten across my chest. "Why would you say that?"

She laughs and does a cute little snort. "Uh, because you didn't ask me to marry you. You felt obligated because of"—she pauses and looks around to make sure no one is within earshot—"the auction. And well, now you're telling people that we're married."

I shrug. "I think I told you once before that I never do things I don't want to do."

She throws her hands up in the air. "Fine, then whatever. If you're not going to take..." Her voice trails off when I give her the look. The one that says if she mentions money again I'm going to lay her over my lap and spank her pretty ass. "if we're going to do this then I need to start doing some wifely duties."

My cock instantly comes alive. I almost reach down and adjust myself, but I figure that would be too obvious. Instead, with a grunt, I ask her, "What do you have in mind?"

She shrugs, lost in thought and completely oblivious to the state of my dick right now. "I don't know. I hired a nurse to stay with Dad some. I can work on your ranch."

Fuck, I don't like the sound of that at all. There's no way I'm going to let her work side by side with Jake. "Stay away from my barn and my cows."

She huffs, offended. "I'm a perfectly capable rancher, Cole. I can work just as hard as any man you have working here."

I nod in agreement because I know she's right. But that's not why I don't want her working my ranch. "Yeah, and none of my hands will get anything done because they'll be too busy trying to get into your pants. Forget it, sweetheart. It's not happening."

She looks between the barn and back at me. "No one wants to get into my pants."

I can't keep the smirk off my face. "I beg to differ. What else you got? What other wifely duty do you want to perform for me?"

Her eyes blink at me, full of innocence. She's not catching on to my innuendo. "I can cook."

I shake my head. "Do you want to put Tina out of a job?" I know Sassy well enough to know she knows Tina has been cooking for my family for a long time. I also know that Sassy would never take someone else's livelihood.

"I can clean, then." I open my mouth, and she holds her hand up. "I know, Tina cleans too. But this place is huge. I'm sure she'd appreciate the help."

I dip my head, shaking it side to side.

I can see her mind racing, trying to think of something. Meanwhile, I'm thinking of all the wifely duties I'd like her to perform. Hell, she wouldn't have to do much. She can just lie back on my bed and let me love every part of her body and I'd be a happy man. All the things I've dreamed about and told myself I'd never have. That's what I want from her. But I can't ask her for it. Not yet. Not until we're past the point where she feels she owes me. She doesn't owe me a damn thing. The things I want from her, I need her to want to give me.

She licks her lower lip, and I suck in a breath. "Fine. Tell me then, Cole. What do you want me to do?"

# SASSY

With a slight hesitation, he answers me. "We can go back to before if that's what you want."

I suck in a breath because it feels like I've been punched in the gut. Is that what he wants? Does he want to forget any of this happened? "Get a divorce? Is that what you want?"

He doesn't answer me at first. He levels me with a stare, and when I start to fidget, he says. "No, we're not getting divorced. I mean, we can go back to the way it was before. Friends."

*Don't say it. Don't say it.* I tell myself that over and over, but I'm not the best listener because the words tumble out of my mouth in a blur. "That doesn't even make sense. So we stay married... but be friends. So you want to relieve your guilty conscience when you go into Jasper and meet up with Delilah to satisfy your needs. Is that it?"

His stare drills into me. "What do you know about Delilah?"

I smirk as if it doesn't bother me. As if the thought of him with another woman doesn't bother me when in fact it drives me insanely jealous. "Everyone knows about the divorcee you meet up with one to two times a month."

He shifts his weight from one foot to the other. "She's a friend."

That doesn't put my mind at ease in the least. He doesn't deny that she satisfies his needs, and that pit in my stomach gets even bigger. "Right. So, friend... I guess if you can have a friend, so can I."

"Over my dead body."

In a strangled voice, I accuse him, "So you are fucking her?"

"No. Yes." He groans. "Look, yes, Delilah and I used to spend time with each other. But we're just friends."

My voice cracks because I don't know if I want to hear the answer or not. "Like friends with benefits?"

He takes a step toward me. "I haven't slept with her in years."

I scrunch my nose up at him. "Years?"

He nods and shrugs his shoulders. "Why are we talking about this?"

I tilt my head back to peer at his face. "Because you want to go back to the way things were before we got married. Which makes no sense to me. You weren't obligated to marry me or anything. It was an OPTION. But whatever, it's done. Now we just need to navigate where to go from here."

I take a few steps away from him and lean against the fence in front of me. I look out at the mountains and take it all in. I get lost in thought as I try to figure this all out. He acts as if he doesn't want to be married to me, but he also makes a point to claim me at every moment. I chance a look at him over my shoulder, and he's staring at my ass. I turn away, and a thrill goes over me. After that kiss, after the way he pleasured me the other night, there's no denying he wants me.

I grab my truck keys out of my pocket and dangle them between my fingers before turning to face him. "I guess we'll just need to figure things out, Cole. We're married, and you're wanting to go back to the way things were before. I'm not going to live my life as a virgin."

I wait for my words to sink in, and it's apparent he's not happy about it by the look that registers on his face. Before he can answer me, I hold my keys up. "I better go."

It takes him three strides to get in front of me and block my path to my truck. His hand wraps around my elbow. "What does that mean, Sassy?"

I flutter my lashes at him, all wide-eyed and innocent. "Exactly what I said."

I pull my arm from his grip. "I have to go. I'm going to the cattlemen's meeting tonight."

He follows me to the truck and opens my door but positions himself so that I can't get in. "Since when do you go to the cattlemen's meetings?"

His eyes study my face. I know he sees more than he lets on, and there's no hiding it from him. "Since my father has been unable to."

. . .

Emotions float across his face. Pity, possession, and then something else. Something that I can't name but makes me feel that he's about to either kiss me or hold me. Right now, I'd take either. This roller coaster of emotions he has me on is keeping me on my toes. I wait with bated breath for him to touch me, but he doesn't. I point to the inside of my truck. "Can you let me in?"

He takes a step back, but I still have to slide my body along his to get to my seat. His hardness against my softness has me going slowly, enjoying the feel of his body against my own. When I get into my seat, I let out a breath. He's blocking my door, but he moves, holding it open. "I'll pick you up at six."

He shuts the door, and I lean out the window. "What? I can drive-"

He shakes his head and starts to walk away as if the conversation is already over. "I'll pick you up at six."

I watch him walk toward his house, and as I pull around to drive down his driveway, I see him standing on the porch watching me. He doesn't lift a hand and wave, nothing, just watches me as I drive away.

I'm not seeing the whole story with what's happening. That's all I can come up with. He's obviously not thrilled to be married to me, that much is obvious, but he's not said one word about getting a divorce. Heck, at this point we can get an annulment. No, there's more to it, and I'm going to find out what it is. It feels like all my dreams are within reach right now but I can't quite grasp them. But a future with Cole is worth fighting for.

# COLE

It's crazy to think Sassy has lived next door to me all these years. I've forced myself to stay away from her, and now I can't even imagine letting her drive into town by herself. This crazy need to claim her is getting out of hand.

I always go to the cattlemen's meeting. Usually, I pick up Delilah, we have dinner, go to the meeting, and then I take her home. I wasn't lying when I said I hadn't slept with her in years. I haven't. And she really is just a friend, but I can understand why Sassy has a hard time believing it. Small town gossip definitely goes rampant sometimes.

I pull up to Sassy's house at a quarter to six. I make my way to her front door and knock. Amos answers the door, and a big smile comes on his face when he sees me. "Cole, it's good to see you, son. What are you doing here this time of night?"

I smile and walk through the door he's holding open for me. I shake his hand. "Good to see you, Amos. I'm here to pick up Sassy."

Right at that moment, Sassy comes in. "Yeah, we're going into town to get something to eat. Can we bring you anything back, Amos?"

I catch on that she's not wanting to tell Amos about the cattlemen's meeting. It will be weird not seeing him there. But I am caught off guard when she calls him Amos. "What are you doing tonight, Amos?"

He looks grudgingly toward Sassy. "Well, it looks as if I'll have the house to myself tonight finally. I'll probably watch a little television, drink a beer, and maybe go shoot a bit."

"Uh..." I start but don't finish.

Sassy rushes toward me, and all thoughts of Amos drinking and shooting guns vanishes. "We should go... we don't want to be late for dinner."

I nod and say bye to Amos, but he's already got his eyes on the television in front of him. I follow Sassy out the door, and she lets out a breath. "Don't worry, the nurse is here. I've hid all the guns from him, and thanks for not telling him about the cattlemen's meeting. Today is an off day, and I know if he went it may set him off."

I shrug and open the passenger side of my truck for her. "He seemed okay. He knew who I was."

She bites onto her lower lip, and I realize what I just said. Fuck. "Sassy..."

She waves me off. "It's fine. Today he thinks I'm the help." She does a little laugh to try and hide the pain she's feeling.

"Aww, honey."

She holds her hand up to stop me. "No, don't. Don't feel sorry for me. I'm fine."

I nod my head. "I know you are." And because I can't stop myself, I lean in and press my lips to hers.

I back away, and she's looking at me with surprise. I've kissed her before—hell, I've had my tongue in her pussy—but a kiss for comfort surprises her. I'm definitely doing something wrong.

The drive to the meeting doesn't take long. Sassy is quiet most of the ride, and even though she's never been to a cattlemen's meeting before, she fits right in. Almost everyone knows her already, and it's obvious by the way the other people react to her that she's respected in the ranching community.

"Sassy Reid!"

Sassy and I both turn at the man's voice. The only difference is I'm scowling and she's smiling ear to ear. They embrace in a hug, and the man lifts her feet off the floor. It takes everything in me not to pull her out of his arms. "Aaron James. I haven't seen you since we graduated! How is college?"

The man's face turns red. "It was okay but not for me. I made it two years and decided I'd rather come back and help run the family ranch."

Sassy seems excited. "So you're back! I bet your family is happy to have you home."

He shakes his head and opens his mouth just as tonight's speaker announces that we're going to start. Sassy and Aaron mention talking after the meeting, and Sassy sits down next to me, smiling ear to ear.

When she finally looks at me, she seems taken aback by the scowl on my face. She looks around and then asks, "What did I miss? You okay?"

I force my eyes off her and to the front of the room. I feel her shrug her shoulders and do the same. She has no idea that just seeing her hugging an old friend is enough to make me come unglued. I've never been a jealous person, but with Sassy, I'm learning all kinds of new things about myself.

Sassy pulls a notebook and pencil out of her purse, and I watch as she focuses on the speakers at the front. I usually pay attention at these things, but Sassy's nearness and the scent of her strawberry shampoo has me off kilter.

The speaker talks about the price of beef, new testing for local water sources, and the current state of hay after the small drought we had, and Sassy writes it all down.

The door behind us bangs, and everyone in their seat turns around. It's Delilah, and she smiles and waves as she comes in the room. "Sorry, everyone. Didn't mean to interrupt or be late. My usual ride bailed on me."

She finds me in the room and smirks at me. I know she's only joking, and I shake my head at her. She comes to my aisle and passes Sassy and then me to sit in the vacant seat next to me. I feel Sassy tense, and I do my best to pay attention to the front of the room, but it's useless. It's like I can see the exact moment that Sassy makes the connection of who the woman is sitting next to me.

Sassy turns to look at me, and Delilah smiles at her, leaning across me with her hand on my knee. "Hey, you must be Sassy. The reason I lost my ride tonight." She laughs as she says it. "I'm Delilah."

All the blood seems to drain from Sassy's face. She grimaces and turns back toward the front. Fuck me, this can't get any worse. I know there's nothing between Delilah and me besides friendship, and she didn't mean anything by it, but obviously Sassy is hurt.

I turn to her. "Sassy, honey..."

She clenches her eyes shut and shakes her head, whispering, "Don't... please."

I slam my mouth shut and try to pay attention the rest of the meeting. Delilah is looking apologetic, Sassy is looking as if she wants to be anywhere but here, and I'm caught in the middle. As soon as the meeting is over, Sassy is on her feet making her way to the door. I reach for her, but she shrugs me off. "I need to go to the ladies' room."

I let her go, and Delilah follows me out of the row. "I guess I shouldn't have opened my damn mouth. I'm sorry, Cole. I didn't mean..."

I shake my head. "It's fine. I'll explain to Sassy."

She nods, squeezes me on the arm, and makes her way across the room. I stare at the door that Sassy went out of and decide to follow her. I go down the hall and wait outside the ladies' bathroom.

There's no one in the hallway and I stand out here for a good five minutes before finally knocking on the door and pushing it open a little. "Sassy? You okay in there?"

Silence.

I push the door open farther. "Sassy!"

When no one answers, I walk in and look under the stalls and see no feet. "Fuck!"

I open my phone and call her. She doesn't answer.

I text her. *Sassy, where are you at?*

I go down the hall and outside. She's not waiting by my truck. I look up and down the street and nothing. She's not walking, and she couldn't have gotten far. I call her again, but she doesn't answer. Then I text her. *Sassy, please, I'm worried. Where are you?*

I wait just a few seconds and text her again. *Please.*

Finally, the bubbles light up, and I let out a breath of relief. If she's texting me, she's at least physically okay. *I got a ride from Aaron. You can now give Delilah a ride home.*

Fuck me! I fucked this up.

I'm in my truck and heading toward home in an instant.

I run red lights and stop signs, and by the time I get on the open road toward our ranches, I floor it. I pull into her driveway with gravel flying.

When I stop, I see Aaron James sitting on Sassy's porch drinking what looks like a glass of iced tea.

I'm out of the truck and up on the porch in an instant. "Hey there, thanks for giving Sassy a ride home."

He's oblivious to what's going on. Sassy is sitting on the porch swing, eyeing me warily while Aaron drinks his tea. He swallows. "Sure thing, no problem."

Because I don't know any other way, I go and sit down next to Sassy on the swing. "Did you tell Aaron our good news?"

She gives me the look. Something like a cross between *How dare you?* and *You'd better not,* but I don't listen because right now, I want the whole damn town to know, and if I have to tell each person I come across, I'll do it. "Sassy and I got married a few days ago."

Aaron chokes on the sweet tea. Sassy makes a move to help him, and I get up and slap him on the back. "You okay?"

He chokes again. "Uh yeah, no, Sassy didn't tell me the good news. Congratulations."

I sit back down and smile at him under the porch light. "Thanks. We appreciate that."

Aaron doesn't hang out after that. He finishes off his tea and makes an excuse to leave before he hightails it out of here.

As soon as he's in his truck, Sassy turns to me with her eyes raging and her hands held tightly together in her lap. "You're telling everyone we're married."

"We are," I deadpan.

She crosses her arms over her chest. "Oh yeah? Did you tell Delilah?"

# SASSY

I regret saying it as soon as I open my mouth. "You know what? Forget it, I don't care."

Cole turns in his seat, stopping the motion of the swing. "You're jealous."

I roll my eyes but don't answer him. Why do I feel like I'm being played or made a fool of? "It doesn't matter."

He puts his hand on my knee. "Sassy, honey, it does matter. I don't want you to feel insecure or jealous. I married you, and yes, I told Delilah. She was happy for us."

I look at him with sadness. "This isn't a real marriage, Cole."

He squeezes my leg. "I have a paper that says otherwise."

"You didn't have to…"

He grabs on to my hands with both of his. "I told you I don't do anything I don't want to do."

I tilt my head and watch him closely. "So you want to be married to me?"

He seems as if he's searching for an answer or trying to figure out what to say. He's surely not admitting his undying love to me. I hold my sigh in and shake my head, overwhelmed with emotion.

He tilts my chin up. "What's that? Right there, what's that look about?"

I pull my chin from his grasp and look at my hands. "Maybe you shouldn't have come to the auction."

"Don't say that. You don't mean that."

"You want to be friends… I want more."

He rubs his hand across my shoulder. My nipples pebble, and goosebumps form on my arm. "I came to the auction because I couldn't let you leave with someone else."

My eyes lift to his, searching for the truth. "Why? Can you tell me why? I can handle the truth, Cole. Is it because you respect my dad? Because you've known me forever? Because I'm like a little sister to you? What is it?"

He laughs darkly. "I definitely don't think of you as a little sister."

"Then why?"

He reaches for me, but I pull away. He looks at me patiently and pats his lap. "Sit here."

"You want me to sit in your lap?"

He nods. "Yeah, I have some things to tell you, and I'd rather do it with you in my arms."

I should be embarrassed that I don't hesitate, but I'm not. I stand up, and his hands go to my waist, pulling me to his lap. He turns me sideways so that his arm supports my back and my legs are up in the seat I just got up from. "Okay."

He lets out a deep breath. "I'm fourteen years older than you, Sassy."

My forehead creases. "So you think I'm too young for you?"

He shakes his head. "I didn't say that." He kisses my forehead. "I did this all wrong. I fucked it up."

His words have me freezing up in his lap, and I try to pull away, but his arms tighten around me. "Hear me out. I should have claimed you the day you turned eighteen. All this time I told myself that you deserved more than me and I stayed away. Then this stupid auction happened. I took complete advantage of you and pretty much forced you into marriage. Hell, I would have given you the money – I wanted to – but when I found out about the auction, I thought I could finally have everything I want."

I almost can't believe what he's saying. He leans his face against mine and whispers into my ear, "You, Sassy. You're what I want."

I gasp and repeat his words to me. "You want me?"

He grunts. "Fuck, more than anything. Why do you think I married you? But here's the deal. Once you're mine, I'm not giving you up. I want a real marriage with you, and there's no turning back because I know I'll never be able to give you up."

He leans in and presses his lips to mine. I still can't believe what he's saying. Cole Rogers wants me. His kiss leaves me breathless, and when he pulls away, he brings us both to our feet. He kisses me again and then lets go of me, moving across the porch. I stare after him with my mouth hanging open. Is he leaving?

He turns and smiles at me. For the first time ever, Cole looks unsure about something. "I need you to be sure, Sass. I need you to choose me because you want to be with me. Not because you feel like you owe me anything. You know where to find me. I'll be waiting for you."

It takes everything I have not to jump off this porch and follow him.

# COLE

Two days I've waited and not a word from Sassy. I'm pretty sure my crew is about to quit and find somewhere else to work. Either that or kill me off in my sleep. I've been an ass even more than normal, and I know I'm taking it out on my men.

Fuck! Today I rode out on the ranch to mend some fences. I needed something to keep me busy, and fixing fence line on a thousand acre ranch will do just that.

By midday, I'm covered in sweat, every muscle in my body hurts, I'm hungry, and I'm still thinking about Sassy.

By the time I start riding home, it's already getting dark. I'm walking Zeus to the barn when Jake comes out. He looks me up and down with a huge smile on his face, and it pisses me off even more. I still haven't quite gotten over him hitting on Sassy. "What?" I ask him.

He shrugs. "Did you roll in the mud while you were out there?"

"Har, har. I worked. Maybe you should try it some time."

He doesn't take any offense to what I said. He just laughs some more. "Well, I thought once you came back, you would have worked out some of your aggression. I guess not."

"Fuck you," I answer and go to walk past him.

He's smirking at me and holds his hand out to take the reins from me. "Here, I'll take care of Zeus."

I don't release my hold on him. "I got him."

Jake crosses his arms over his chest. "I just thought since your wife was up at the house, you'd want to go see her, but okay."

I give him the look that tells him he better not be fucking with me. "Sassy's here?"

He nods. "Yep, showed up earlier. I let her in. You really should give your wife a key-"

I cut him off and throw the reins at him. "Thanks for taking care of Zeus. Rub him down; he worked hard today."

I'm sprinting through the barn as I tell him what to do. I come out the other side that has a view of the house, and sure enough, Sassy's truck is sitting in the driveway. I run up to the house and stop on the porch to catch my breath. Smoothing my hands down my chest, I look down at myself covered in dirt, mud, and sweat. Fuck, this is not what I had planned.

I open the front door and hold my breath as I walk through the house. Finally, I find her in the kitchen, washing dishes. I could stand here all night and watch her, but when she turns off the water, I say her name.

She jerks, surprised to see me standing here. "Cole."

I take a step forward. "Hey, Sass." For the first time ever, she's wearing a dress, and I can't seem to take my eyes off her legs. "You look beautiful."

She smiles, and the way she fidgets, I can tell she's nervous. "Thank you. Tina went into town to see her sister. I told her I'd make you dinner, but I'll warn you now, I'm not much of a cook. I made some chili."

I'm watching her intently. I have a thousand questions I want to ask, but I don't want to bombard her. "I'm not picky. I'm sure it's good. Do I have time to shower real quick?"

She bites on to her lip and nods. "Sure."

I want to reach for her and kiss her, but I don't. "I'll be right back."

I go down the hall to my bedroom. I strip all my clothes off and take the fastest shower I've ever had. By the time I'm back in a clean pair of jeans and a T-shirt, I'm making my way back down the hall to the kitchen, running my fingers through my hair. She seems surprised when I cut the corner. "That was quick."

I just shrug in response. I don't want to tell her that I was worried she'd leave before I got back out here. She sets a plate of cornbread on the table, and I stop her before she goes back toward the stove. "What took you so long?"

Her eyes widen. "Uh, I had to brown the beef-"

"No, I mean what took you so long to come over here?"

She shrugs. "Well, you said you wouldn't let me go..."

I nod and brush a strand of hair away from her face. "I won't."

She smiles. "Right, well, I had to hire a full-time nurse and talk to Frank and the new hand I hired. I'll have to go over there every day, but I think between Frank and the new guy, it should be okay. Plus, I had to pack."

My body tenses. "You packed?"

Her cheeks turn a pretty pink. "Well, yeah, I mean... I thought.." She seems to pull her shoulders back. "Yes. I packed."

I look down the hallway toward the front door and don't see any bags. I know I didn't see them in my bedroom. Surely she didn't put them in the spare bedroom. "Where are your bags?"

"In my truck."

I release her instantly. "I'll be right back."

"The food..." she calls after me.

I holler over my shoulder, "I'll eat it, I promise. Set it to warm. I have a few things to take care of first."

I walk outside, pleased to see the bed of her truck full of bags. I start carrying them in as she watches me. "I could have brought them in, but I wasn't sure where to put them."

I stop next to her and kiss her lips. "In our bedroom. You're sleeping in my room... in my bed."

She swallows, and her eyes light up with need. "Okay."

I lift her bags up. "Relax. I'll get these."

She doesn't listen, though. She follows me down the hall and watches as I set the bags down on the floor. I open the closet and point to the empty side and then go to the dresser and open the empty drawers. "I made room for all your stuff."

She smiles. "You knew I'd come?"

I shrug, not wanting her to know how worried I was, wondering if she was going to want me or not. "I hoped."

# SASSY

"You hoped I'd come?"

I know I'm being ridiculous. He said he wanted me, but there are still parts of me – the tomboy that's never been good enough – that still wonders if this could possibly be real. And then I remind myself that he paid six million dollars to have me. Surely, that's telling.

Even though I've spent the last two days questioning everything – like how long is this really going to be for, if he's going to get tired of me and he still hasn't said he loved me – I knew that I would come.

Cole comes toward me and puts his hands at my waist. "Your eyes are going wild. Like a caged animal. You want to be here, right, Sass?"

I let out a deep breath. "Yeah, I want to be here. Of course, I want to be here. And I know there are no guarantees, but I'm just thinking when you get tired of me-"

He cuts me off. "Tired of you? Fuck, honey, I'm thinking the same thing about you. I could spend the rest of my days running this ranch with you by my side and I'd be the happiest man on earth. Is that going to be enough for you? You're young, you probably want to travel, to see the world."

I know that I need to just put it out there and let him know. He deserves to know. "Cole, there's probably something you should know."

He tenses but doesn't let me go. "What is it?"

I clench my eyes and open them, forcing myself to look at him. "I've dreamed of this. Being here with you. You were always the one that I pictured when I thought of marrying and having a family. It was always a dream that I thought was out of reach. No, I'll never get tired of being with you. Being with you is like a dream come true."

He grunts and wraps his arms around me, pulling me in against his chest. "Fuck, I love you, Sassy."

I gasp against his chest. "You love me?"

He pulls back to search my face. "Fuck, I've messed this up. I've done nothing right since the beginning, but I'm going to fix it now. I love you, Sassy. I have for what seems like forever. You're the only woman I've ever loved, and I knew I wanted to spend the rest of my life with you."

He swallows and shifts his lower body until his hard bulge is pressed against my belly. "I want everything with you, Sassy."

I nod. "I want that. All of that, Cole. With you. I love you. I have for a long time."

He leans down and presses his lips to mine. My hands slide under his shirt and trail up his chest. His skin seems to vibrate under my touch, but I can't get enough. I run my hands along his muscles, and when I find a hard, pebbled nipple, I trace it with my finger. He groans into my mouth and pulls away. With his eyes searching mine, I find his other nipple and trace it too, smiling up at him.

"I want you, Cole."

His hand comes up to cover mine. "I'm in no rush, honey. I want you. Fuck, I want you, but as long as you sleep in that bed with me – as long as you're mine – I can wait."

I pull my hands from his and grab the hem of his shirt. I pull it up his body, and he has to lean over with his arms up to help me take it off. I can't take my eyes off him. I've seen him without his shirt on before, but up close where I can touch him is like nothing I've ever experienced before. "I want you."

I say it clearly, and there's no doubt he heard me. His whole body seems to flex under my hands. I slide my hands down his waist and grab the button of his jeans. "I want you, Cole."

His smirk is fast and sudden, causing me to catch my breath. My, he's handsome. "I'm yours, baby. All yours."

I bite my lower lip as I undo the button and pull the zipper down. I've come this far, and there's no stopping now. He stands perfectly still as I grab onto his waistband and pull the material down, gasping his hard cock when it springs free.

He's hard... for me.

I sit on my legs just looking at him up close. Without thinking, I reach for him, wrapping my hand around his girth. He groans, and his hands go to my shoulders as his hips jerk backwards. My mouth falls open. "Cole! I'm sorry... did I hurt you?"

He moans and stands back upright. "No, baby, I just wasn't prepared. I didn't realize..."

His voice trails off, and I blink up at him, wide-eyed and not understanding. "If I'm doing it wrong, you have to tell me. I want to do it right. I want to make you feel good."

His hand goes to the nape of my neck. "You can't do anything wrong."

I roll my eyes and put my hands on his bare thighs. "Cole! Tell me."

He wraps one hand around his girth and squeezes it. His voice is gruff. "I'm telling you the truth. You can't do anything wrong. Not with me. The reason I pulled away is because it's too much... having you here on your knees and your mouth and hands on me... it's too much. I'm going to come."

I lick my lips and ask him, "Isn't that the point? Don't you want to?"

He leans over and pulls me up until I'm standing in front of him. His hand slides down the front of my dress. He pulls my hem up and lays his hand against the apex of my thighs. "Yeah, honey, I want to come, but when I do, I want to be here."

My hips flex, and he rubs his palm against me. I grab on to his forearms as I lift up to get closer. "I want that too."

He slides his hand into the waistband of my underwear, and when his finger touches my bare skin, my body trembles. His finger slides through my wet slit, and I hold on to his arm as if it's a lifeline. The things he's doing to my body makes me feel things I've never felt before. His voice is gruff next to my ear. "You're so wet, baby. You want this, don't you? Want me to come in that pretty pussy of yours?"

I wasn't prepared for the dirty talk, and it forms a knot in my lower belly. "Yes, please, Cole. I need it... I need you."

# COLE

Her desperate pleas for more has me gripping her dress and pulling it off her body. I waste no time in helping her out of her bra and panties. When she's bare before me, I lift her up and lay her back on the bed. Her legs fall open, and her glistening wet slit is beckoning me. First my hands slide up her thighs, pushing them farther apart.

I lean in, kissing her inner thigh, making my way to her honeyed core.

Her moans fill the air as I suck her clit between my lips. With her hands in my hair and her hips lifting to meet me, I lap at her, savoring her taste on my tongue.

She's already so close, and I'm about to take her over the edge when she sits up, grabbing my arms and pulling me toward her. I'm stronger than her, but I don't resist as she pulls me over top of her. I try to keep as much of my weight as I can off of her, but it doesn't seem to bother her because she's wrapping her legs around my waist, pulling me tightly against her.

I suckle her breast, licking her nipple, and she moans. I can't get enough, and between licks, I ask her, "Why'd you make me stop?"

When she doesn't answer me, I lift up to look in her eyes. Her eyes are filled with desire and darker than just minutes before. "I want to come with you inside me, Cole, and I was close."

My hips jerk, and she smiles. Already she knows the control she has over me. She reaches between us and wraps her hand around my hard manhood. She grips me tightly and brings her hand from my root to my tip. Cum seeps from my tip, and when she feels the moisture on her hand, she smears it along my length. "Fuck," I groan.

I pull away from her and sit on my knees between her thighs. I wrap one hand around my girth and run my fingers on my other hand between her spread thighs.

"I'm taking you bare. I'm going to come deep inside you."

Her hand goes to my chest. She acts as if she can't stand not touching me, and everywhere she can reach, her hand is caressing my body. "I'm not on the pill."

With a grunt, I raise up and position myself at her core. "Good."

We don't talk about it, but the way her eyes search mine, I know she realizes that she may get pregnant... that I want her pregnant. Even though I want it, I still ask, "You okay with that?"

She nods. "Yeah, I'd like that."

More cum oozes from my tip, and I paint her pussy with my arousal. I push into her, inch by inch. She's so tight, I stop and try to get ahold of myself before I come too soon. She's impatient, though, and shifts her hips, lifting up and pushing me deeper inside her.

"Please don't stop, Cole."

I put a hand on her lower belly and hold her down. "I don't want to hurt you."

She shakes her head. "You won't. I need you... please."

I take a deep breath and push inside her, burying myself into her honeyed depths. I watch her face closely, and she grimaces, but just as quickly, a smile forms on her lips. I stop when I'm buried to the hilt and I don't know where I end and she begins. "You okay?"

I can feel sweat beading on my forehead as I try to hold still when everything inside me is saying to move. She reaches up, cupping my face, running her finger along my lower lip. "Yeah, Cole. I'm good... Love me, please."

I can't resist her. I lift out of her and plunge back in. Over and over, I thrust into her. She fits me like she was made for me. I'm so close, and I roll onto my back, taking her with me. She screams and then laughs as she's seated on my thighs, my cock still buried inside her.

"What... why?"

I grab on to her hips, sliding her front to back. "I want you to ride me."

She scrunches up her nose. "I don't know how... what do I do?"

She moves her hips, but she's hesitant. I lift my hips, and she moans as she grinds her pussy down on to me. My voice is lust-filled. "Do what makes you feel good."

She moves her hips front to back and then side to side. "But what about you?"

I hold back a chuckle. "Trust me, honey, anything you do is going to feel good to me."

She puts her hands on my chest and moves back and forth. She leans forward, grinding her clit into me and then leans back so my cock is hitting her at a different angle. Her body shudders, and I swear her pussy gets wetter and hotter.

I lift up. "You like that, don't you?"

She moans, and her whole body trembles. "Yes."

I thrust up, meeting her, and she starts to move uncontrollably. Her hands grip on to me painfully, but it doesn't stop me. "Oh...oh..." she says, and I know she's about to come.

I reach down and rub my finger in circles around her clit. Her body starts to convulse on top of me. She's writhing, but I'm holding her steady as my own orgasm shoots through my body. She has my cock in a vise, milking me, but she doesn't stop until there are only slight tremors vibrating against my manhood. She falls onto my chest, and I let out an oomph as she takes my breath away. We're both sweaty, and I brush the hair off her face, looking into the eyes of the woman that claimed my heart and now my body too.

"I love you."

Her smile is soft. "I love you, too."

It's not enough, though. I lean down and kiss her forehead. "You're mine, now, Sassy. Forever."

She lays her head on my chest. Her eyes have closed, but she's smiling. "Forever… I like the sound of that."

# Epilogue

## Cole

Three Months Later

My wife left early this morning, and by midafternoon, I'd had enough. I'm used to having her by my side either here or at her dad's ranch, so when she isn't home by midafternoon, I decide to go looking for her.

I drive over to her dad's ranch and take it all in as I pull up the driveway. There's been a lot of changes in the last three months. Everything she wanted to do for her dad, we've done together. His ranch is striving again and making money. But probably the best thing is that we finally convinced him to go see a specialist in Jasper. He's doing better, or at least having more good days than bad, and that makes Sassy happy. When Sassy's happy, I'm happy. That's all there is to it.

When I pull my truck up next to the house, I see Sassy and Amos sitting on the porch. They both smile and wave at me. "There's my son-in-law. I wondered how long it would take you to come looking for her."

I laugh at Amos. I had worried when we told him that we were married. He of course doesn't know any of the details about the auction or anything like that, but I still thought he would not be happy with our age difference and everything. But he surprised me. He was pretty happy to find out that he had a son-in-law and that son-in-law was me. I walk up the porch and sit next to my pretty wife, who is sipping on a sweet tea. "You know I can't stay away from her long. I was missing her for sure."

He nods his head. We talk about the ranch and the order of supplies that was delivered today. The whole time, I'm thinking I can't wait to get my wife back home and in our bed.

Amos stands up. "Well, I'm going to go out to the barn and see how Frank's doing with the inoculations. I'll catch you two later."

Sassy stops him before he gets off the porch. "Dad, we're going to head home soon, but I thought maybe one night this week we can get together for dinner. You up for it?"

He puts his hand to his stomach and looks at Sassy. "You cooking or Tina cooking?"

"Har, har," she says jokingly. "Keep it up, and I'll tell Tina to stop making your favorite apple pie."

His mouth falls open, and he holds his hands up. "No, don't do that. You name the day and time, and I'll be there."

She laughs. "That's better. Love you, Dad."

He looks at Sassy and me and walks over to us. He kisses his daughter on the top of the head. "Love you too, Sassy." With a grip on my shoulder, he says, "Love you too, son. Thanks for making my girl so happy."

I'm speechless as he walks off the porch and to the barn. Sassy pokes me in the ribs. "You okay?"

I look at her. "Uh, did your dad just tell me he loved me?"

She nods, searching my face. "He did. It's been a good day."

I gather her in my arms and pull her onto my lap. "Well, I'm glad you've had a good day. Mine hasn't been the best."

She puts her hands on my shoulders and looks at me worriedly. "Oh no, Cole. What happened? Are you okay?"

I shrug. "I missed you, that's all."

She pulls back, surprised. "You missed me? I figured you were getting sick of me at this point. I thought I needed to give you a break from me following you around on your ranch."

I shake my head. "Nope. I like having you with me. It's weird when you're not there... You've made it a home, Sassy. It's not the same without you."

She smiles and curls into my lap. It seems that neither one of us is in a hurry to move. I'm content to stay right here as long as I'm holding my wife.

She sighs contently. "There's something I should tell you."

I run my fingers through the soft strands of her hair. "What's that?"

She sits up and searches my face. I try to read her expression, but all I see is a mixture of emotions ranging from excitement to fear. "What is it?" I ask her when she doesn't answer me fast enough.

She reaches for my hand and picks it up, placing it on her belly. I press my palm there as she starts to tell me, "I went to the doctor this morning. You're going to be a daddy."

"What? You're pregnant? We're pregnant?" I ask her excitedly.

She nods as a tear rolls down her face. She looks relieved. "I guess you're excited."

I cup her face with my hands. "Oh baby, I didn't think I could be any happier, but you proved me wrong. I love you, Sassy."

She pulls from my hold and stands up, holding her hand out. I reach for her without hesitation, and she pulls me to stand up. "Now let's go home and celebrate."

I pull her up into my arms and stride down the porch to my truck. We can come get hers later. I don't want to be away from her. It's only when I have her settled in the truck that I look at her and see the happiness on her face. "Who would have thought that when I won that auction, all my dreams would come true?"

She leans in and kisses me until we're both breathless. "Me too, Cole. Me too."

## Also by Hope Ford

Want more of Whiskey Run?

### *Whiskey Run*

Faithful - He's the hot, say-it-like-it-is cowboy, and he won't stop until he gets the woman he wants.

Captivated - She's a beautiful woman on the run... and I'm going to be the one to keep her.

Obsessed - She's loved him since high school and now he's back.

Seduced - He's a football player that falls in love with the small town girl.

Devoted - She's a plus size model and he's a small town mechanic.

### *Whiskey Run: Savage Ink*

Virile - He won't let her go until he puts his mark on her.

Torrid - He'll do anything to give her what she wants.

Rigid - If you love reading about emotionally wounded men and the women that help them overcome their past, then you'll love Dawson and Emily's story.

### *Whiskey Run: Cowboys Love Curves*

Obsessed Cowboy - She's the preacher's daughter and she's off limits.

## *Whiskey Run: Heroes*

Ransom - He's on a mission he can't lose.

Redeem - He's in love with his sister's best friend.

Submit - She's his fake wife but he wants to make it real.

Forbid - They have a secret romance but he's about to stake his claim.

## *Whiskey Run: Sugar*

One Night Love - Her one night stand wants more.

Rebound Love - She's falling for the rebound guy.

Second Chance Love - He is not a man to ignore... especially when he asks for a second chance.

Bad Boy Love - He's a bad boy that wants her good.

## *Whiskey Run: Guardians MC*

Protective Biker - She needs his protection and he'll give it to her. But he's going to need her heart in exchange.

Broken Biker - There's only one woman for him...

Relentless Biker - He won't stop until he has her back.

# JOIN ME!

## JOIN MY NEWSLETTER

www.AuthorHopeFord.com/Subscribe

# BE A HOTTIE!

## JOIN HOPE'S HOTTIES ON FACEBOOK

### www.FB.com/groups/hopeford

A place to talk about Hope Ford's books! Find out about new releases, giveaways, get exclusive content, see covers before anyone else and more!

# About the Author

USA Today Bestselling Author Hope Ford writes short, steamy, sweet romances. She loves tattooed, alpha men, instant love stories, and ALWAYS happily ever afters. She has over 100 books and they are all available on Amazon.

To find me on Pinterest, Instagram, Facebook, Goodreads, and more:

www.AuthorHopeFord.com/follow-me

Want FREE BOOKS?
Go to www.authorhopeford.com/freebies

Printed in Great Britain
by Amazon